Other Little Princess picture books

I Want My Potty
I Want My Dinner
I Want To Be
I Want A Sister
I Don't Want To Go To Hospital
I Want My Dummy
Wash Your Hands
I Want My Tooth!
I Don't Want To Go To Bed

Little Princess Board Books are also available:
Shapes, Weather, Pets, Bedtime,
I Want My Potty, I Want My Dinner,
I Want To Be, I Want A Sister

Copyright © 2004 by Tony Ross
The rights of Tony Ross to be identified as the author and illustrator of this work
have been asserted by him in accordance with the Copyright, Designs and Patents Act, 1988.
First published in Great Britain in 2004 by Andersen Press Ltd, 20 Vauxhall Bridge Road,
London SW1V 2SA. Published in Australia by Random House Australia Pty.,
20 Alfred Street, Milsons Point, Sydney, NSW 2061. All rights reserved.
Colour separated in Switzerland by Photolitho AG, Zürich.
Printed and bound in Italy by Grafiche AZ, Verona.

10   9   8   7   6   5   4   3   2   1

British Library Cataloguing in Publication Data available.

ISBN 1 84270 297 1

This book has been printed on acid-free paper

I Want My Mum!

Tony Ross

Andersen Press
London

It was raining and the Little Princess was busy with
her painting when the awful thing happened . . .

. . . she knocked her water pot over and she spoiled
the best painting she had ever done.

"Don't worry," said the Maid, "everything's OK!"
And she mopped up the mess.
"I WANT MY MUM!" yelled the Little Princess.

Mum held up the soggy picture.
"That's WONDERFUL!" she said. "A rainy day."
The Little Princess smiled.

When the rain stopped, she went outside to play on the see-saw and the terrible thing happened . . .
She banged her knee.

"There, there," said the Doctor. "That's OK now."
And she put some smelly stuff on it.
"I WANT MY MUM!" cried the Little Princess.

And Mum kissed the smelly knee better.
The Little Princess smiled.

That night, the Little Princess couldn't sleep
because of the monster living under the bed.

"There isn't a monster living under the bed,"
said Dad. "Look!" But the Little Princess daren't.
"I WANT MY MUM!" she screamed.

"I'll read stories to you and the monster," said Mum.
The Little Princess smiled. And fell asleep.

"I HATE eggs!" said the Litle Princess at breakfast.
"Eat it up," said the Cook. "It's awfully good for you."
"I WANT MY MUM!" howled the Little Princess.

"Oh, GOODY!" said Mum. "Dinosaur eggs. I love those."
The Little Princess smiled. "Hey, save some for ME!"

All morning the Little Princess had to play by herself.
The Maid popped in to play Snakes and Ladders.
"I WANT MY MUM!" bawled the Little Princess.

The Admiral popped in to play boats.
"I WANT MY MUM!" hooted the Little Princess.

The Little Prince popped in to play anything at all.
And to stop the noise.
"I WANT MY MUM!" shrieked the Little Princess.

At last Mum came, with some thrilling news.
"The Little Duchess has asked you over for a sleepover tonight, with crisps and a video."

The Little Princess packed her bag, and began to cry.
"What's the MATTER?" said Mum.

"I DON'T WANT TO GO!" sobbed the Little Princess.
"I WANT TO STAY HERE WITH GILBERT AND YOU!"
"But Gilbert and I are coming with you," said Mum.

At the Little Duchess's castle, the video was turned on and Mum crept away.
"I WANT MY M . . ." began the Little Princess . . .

. . . but the video was terribly funny,
and the crisps were terribly good . . .

The Little Princess smiled.

Back at the Royal Palace, the Queen was chatting to the King. "She's having a wonderful time," she said. Then . . .

"I WANT MY LITTLE PRINCESS!"